JEREMY BROWN
SECRET SERVICE

Imagine if one of your classmates was really a secret agent like James Bond! Well Jeremy Brown is – and this is the first story about his funny, action-packed adventures!

Simon Cheshire has written stories since he was at school, but it was only after turning thirty that he realized "my mental age would never exceed ten and that, in children's books, I had finally found my natural habitat." He has written three stories about Jeremy Brown – *Jeremy Brown of the Secret Service* (his first published book), *Jeremy Brown and the Mummy's Curse* and *Jeremy Brown on Mars*. The stories, he claims, "are based entirely upon actual events. Only names, characters, plots, dialogue and descriptive content have been changed, to make them more believable." He is also the author of *They Melted His Brain!*, *Totally Unsuitable for Children* and *Dirty Rotten Tricks*.

Books by the same author

Jeremy Brown and the Mummy's Curse
Jeremy Brown on Mars

For older readers

Dirty Rotten Tricks
They Melted His Brain!
Totally Unsuitable for Children

JEREMY BROWN
OF THE
SECRET SERVICE

SIMON CHESHIRE

Illustrations by

HUNT EMERSON

WALKER BOOKS
AND SUBSIDIARIES
LONDON • BOSTON • SYDNEY

To Dawn
for her love and patience

First published 1997 by Walker Books Ltd
87 Vauxhall Walk, London SE11 5HJ

This edition published 2001

2 4 6 8 10 9 7 5 3 1

Text © 1997 Simon Cheshire
Illustrations © 1997, 2001 Hunt Emerson

This book has been typeset in Plantin

Printed and bound in Great Britain
by The Guernsey Press Co. Ltd

British Library Cataloguing in Publication Data:
a catalogue record for this book
is available from the British Library

ISBN 0-7445-7800-0

Contents

Chapter 1

St. Marie's Primary School
Macindoe Crescent
Kirkcaldy
KY1 2JH

In which Jeremy Brown nearly gets duffed up

Jeremy Brown had a secret. His mum didn't know what it was, his dad didn't know what it was, and neither did his younger sisters. Patsy Spudd, his best friend from school, she knew all about it, but she was sworn to secrecy, cross her heart and hope to die.

However, things will get pretty confusing if his secret isn't revealed here and now. Jeremy Brown was an MI7 agent. His boss at MI7 reckoned Jeremy was pretty excellent when it came to foiling evil plots of international proportions. And so did Jeremy. Mind you, his missions were never accomplished easily.

It was a Tuesday, and the weather was grumpy. Jeremy Brown was on his way to school, swinging his bag and watching the clouds grumbling around the sky. He was quite short, quite scruffy, and quite unable to see properly without his glasses, and he didn't notice Sharkface until he walked right slap-bang into him. Jeremy bounced back and landed with a thud on the pavement. Sharkface didn't. Sharkface stayed exactly where he was.

His name wasn't really Sharkface, of course. His name was Mark, but Mark rhymed with shark, and his strange, long nose made his head look sort of wedge-shaped. Even then, people might not have called him Sharkface had it not been for the fact that he was the nastiest bully in the school.

Nervous rays of sunlight crossed Jeremy's face (and his glasses). He couldn't run away, because Sharkface would chase him and duff him up. He couldn't stay where he was, because Sharkface would simply duff him up there and then. Either way, he was going to get his blazer torn. The situation looked hopeless. The situation wasn't really hopeless, as you might guess from the title of this chapter, but Jeremy felt hopeless anyway.

"Brown," said Sharkface, nastily.

Jeremy felt like saying, "What a wonderful memory for names you have, Sharkface," but he didn't. It would only have made Sharkface angry. So instead, he made a sort of whimpering noise, which was more in line with what Sharkface expected.

"I don't like you, Brown. You're a little weed with specs," he said, even more nastily.

"I–I just want to get to school," said Jeremy, as bravely as the situation would allow, which wasn't very bravely at all, to be honest.

"I got an idea," said Sharkface, in the nastiest way possible. If he'd been a cartoon character, a light bulb would have appeared in a think bubble above him. "I'm going to turn you upside down and bounce you on your head." He smiled, and the effect was horrible.

He reached down with both thick, meaty fists, and lifted Jeremy off his feet. He pulled him up close. Jeremy could smell salt and vinegar crisps on Sharkface's breath. He felt something go tight in his throat. Then the same something went tight in his stomach. He braced himself and gritted his teeth.

Suddenly, there was a flash of ginger hair, and the swoosh of a school bag being swung through the air. The bag whopped Sharkface in the stomach, and he dropped Jeremy, who found himself back on the pavement, staring at the sky.

"Oh no, it's Patsy Spudd!" Sharkface moaned.

"What a wonderful memory for names you have, Sharkface," said Patsy.

That made Sharkface angry. He leaped at Patsy with a rumbling grunt. Patsy dodged quickly, and he toppled into a tangle of tree-trunk arms and legs in the gutter.

Patsy stood over him, with her freckle-dotted nose in the air. Or, rather, she stood next to him, since he was at least twice her height, even when he was in a tangle of arms and legs in the gutter.

"Pick on someone your own size," said Patsy loftily. "Come on, Jeremy." She helped him up and they ran.

Sharkface watched them for a moment, with his mouth wriggling into a sneer. It was his way of trying to look tough when he knew perfectly well that he looked silly.

As soon as they were out of his sight, Patsy gave Jeremy a kick on the shin.

"Ow!" yelped Jeremy. "What was that for?"

"Relying on me to rescue you," said Patsy grumpily.

"I keep telling you, I can't blow my cover," whispered Jeremy. "Brilliantly clever and highly trained agents like me must stay in the shadows. I have to pretend to be Sharkface-food at all times."

In his office, the Headmaster was carefully folding an origami elephant. The Headmaster was very round, with a very red face and stubby, sausage-like fingers, but he folded his paper models with great delicacy and skill.

The little finger on each hand pointed outwards as he completed the creature's trunk.

The *bbbbrrrr-ttttrrrr* of the phone made him jump. He twirled in his enormous chair, and the last wisps of grey hair that clung to his head twirled with him.

"Yes! Headmaster!" he barked.

"No, *you're* the Headmaster," said the voice on the phone.

The Headmaster sat up suddenly, and his origami elephant spun to the floor. He'd heard this voice before. His face went a purply shade of mauve.

"Now listen here!" he snapped. "I don't know who you are, but you're not getting me to let Brown and Spudd off school again!"

"Then I presume," said the voice softly, "you don't mind if the whole world finds out that you wear underpants with Frank the Cuddly Bunny on them?"

A purply shade of mauve was no longer good enough. The Headmaster went white.

"H–H–How…? How did you…? I'll have their letters of authorization ready in ten minutes."

To find out whose voice that was, Jeremy and Patsy's history lesson with Mr Plantaganet will have to be interrupted. This won't bother either of them one little bit.

Just as they were busy not paying attention to the details of the Industrial Revolution, Jeremy's left thumb began to tingle. Either he'd accidentally bashed it with a hammer (not very likely in the middle of double History), or he was about to get an important message.

"Sir!" he yelled. "Sir! Got to go to the toilet!"

The rest of the class giggled, except Patsy, who realized what was up.

"Can't it wait, Brown?" said Mr Plantaganet.

"No, sir! Bursting!" Jeremy jigged about a bit in his chair for added effect. Mr Plantaganet waved a weary hand and Jeremy dashed from the room.

Out in the corridor, he activated the communicator hidden under his left thumbnail. It was a silly place to have hidden it, because pulling out the miniature aerial always hurt.

"Ooo, ow!"

The earpiece was concealed under his right thumbnail. He spoke into his left thumb, with his right thumb jabbed into his ear. He put on a very serious expression and gave his identification code: "MI7, the custard is banana flavoured."

"With fruit portions," said the voice. "Pay attention. This is Control. Three days ago, the Com-Star communications satellite developed a fault and dropped out of orbit. It will crash somewhere in your sector in approximately fifteen minutes. It's designed to withstand impact, so it should land in one piece. It's roughly the size and shape of a dustbin. Your mission is to retrieve it, before anyone else does."

"Anyone else?" muttered Jeremy, slightly worried.

"It contains experimental computers which are years ahead of their time, stuff that any of the world's worst villains would pay millions for."

The bell rang, doors opened, and the corridor was suddenly filled with the sounds of clattering feet and chattering voices. Patsy appeared as Jeremy quickly pushed the miniature aerial back into place.

"Ooo, ow!"

"Are we off?" said Patsy excitedly.

"We're off," said Jeremy. And off they went.

As they left the building, the Headmaster came running up to them, puffing and panting. Trembling, he gave them each a letter of permission to be out of school. He had a helpless grin on his face, and kept dabbing a hankie to his forehead.

"Here you are. Er, have a nice time," he said, and quickly wobbled back to his office.

"You don't suppose he suspects?" whispered Patsy.

"No, he doesn't suspect," said Jeremy, with a grin.

They hurried to the school gates, and Jeremy told her about the message from HQ.

"How can they be sure it's going to fall somewhere around here?" said Patsy.

"Well, er, they'll have followed its trajectory ... thingummy. Or something," said Jeremy, who paid even less attention in Maths than he did in History.

Now it was time to set off on another daring, dangerous, deadly and other-things-beginning-with-'d' mission, it was also time for Jeremy to smarten himself up. Being quite short, quite scruffy and quite unable to see without his glasses was just a disguise. Suddenly he stood up straight, did up his shoelaces, and popped his glasses into his top pocket.

"At last," he said with a sigh, pulling up his tie properly and making his eyes go all narrow and tough-looking. "I do so hate having to look scruffy."

Patsy, on the other hand, was quite happy to be her normal self, ketchup-stained and looking like she'd been dragged through a hedge backwards.

"Come on," she said. "We haven't got long."

Chapter 2

In which an evil scheme is hatched, and a satellite drops to Earth

....

Meanwhile, on the other side of town, in an abandoned factory, deep in the remains of a damp and musty basement, three of the country's most notorious and despicable villains were practising their French.

"Vooz ett ern ... cosh-on trez gross," said Kenneth. He was almost two and a half metres tall, with shoulders like a couple of medium sized sheep fighting under a blanket, and a face like a bulldog that's been chewing a wasp. As he read the words, he followed them on the page with a grubby thumb. "You are a very fat pig."

"Vooz ett ern cosh-on trez gross," repeated his brother, who looked exactly the same and, by a strange twist of fate, was also called Kenneth. Their mum had been a terribly confused woman.

Neither of them was worried that their pronunciation was terrible. They were reading an article entitled "How To Insult People In Thirteen Languages", which appeared in the new issue of *Thug!*, the club magazine of ROTTEN (the Rancid Organization for Terror, Threats, Evil and Nastiness).

The third villain, a tall and wiry man with a tall and wiry moustache, stepped out of the shadows. His name was Sid Lime, and his eyes appeared to have been borrowed from one of those paintings which follow you around the room in creepy old houses. "Amateurs," he spat with a growl.

"We're expund— expind— we're biggering our education," said Kenneth and Kenneth together. First-Kenneth scratched his head, and Second-Kenneth scratched his bottom.

"Listen," hissed Sid quietly. He didn't need to hiss quietly, because there was nobody for miles around, but he reckoned it was a more villainous thing to do. "Listen, you micro-brained dollops of chimp poo. While you've been eating extra bananas to get enough skins to slip under the feet of old ladies, some of us have been doing serious research."

With a flourish of paper, he flicked open his copy of *Wrong Doer*, the newsletter of SCUM. (SCUM was the Society of Criminals; the U and the M didn't stand for anything, but SC didn't sound like much on its own.)

"There! Read the headline!"

First-Kenneth mouthed the words carefully. " 'I Lied, Confesses Frankenstein – Monster Was Man In Suit!' "

"No, above that," said Sid.

" 'Five Minutes To Go Until Satellite Hits Town – Dash For Computer Secrets Is On!' "

Sid folded the newspaper with a couple of lightning movements and stuffed it into his pocket. "By the end of the day, gentlemen, we will be richer than a millionaire in a thick chocolate sauce. Move out!"

Sid marched towards the stairs, cackling in

the high-pitched manner approved by the official SCUM handbook. Kenneth and Kenneth followed, giggling excitedly.

Sid's voice echoed around the dripping, shadowy walls. "Hurry, gentlemen, I estimate that the satellite will appear in the sky any second now!"

"Patsy, I estimate that the satellite will appear in the sky any second now," said Jeremy, peering through his binoculars and tapping his pocket calculator. They were standing on the corner of the high street, getting funny looks from shoppers.

"Whereabouts?" said Patsy, looking up and leaning back as far as she dared.

"Umm, up there somewhere, definitely." He tapped at his pocket calculator a bit more.

"I'd say," said Patsy thoughtfully, "that it'll appear as a small red streak of flame, visible on a direct line from this spot past the roof of the greengrocer's."

Jeremy stopped tapping and looked at her,

eyes wide. "That's a remarkably precise and confident prediction," he said. "How can you know that?"

"Because there's a small red streak of flame visible on a direct line from this spot past the roof of the greengrocer's."

Jeremy whirled around and looked at the red streak through the binoculars for a moment. "Now, judging from the angle of descent (*tap – tap – tap – tap*) and the speed of motion (*tap – tap – tap – tap*), and all that kind of stuff, we can calculate that it will land in (*tap*), crumbs, Brazil!"

Patsy snatched the calculator from him. "Oh, give it here." She did her own sums. "It's coming down somewhere near the sewage works," she mumbled.

"Oh, *yuk!*" cried Jeremy. "I'll get *filthy!*"

Patsy consulted her fold-out map of the town. "Ah, no, not the sewage works..."

"Thank goodness for that."

"It's going to land on the school."

"WHAT?!"

"Exactly!" cried Patsy, flipping her hair out of her eyes. "It'll have to be evacuated!"

"No," said Jeremy, "I mean, 'What? We've got to go all the way back there again?' It's miles. Did I ever tell you about the time I was blasted 476 kilometres into space by a pair of exploding underpants?"

"Many times," said Patsy wearily.

They set off for the school. Jeremy hoped that, whatever happened, they didn't come face to face with a gang of desperate, greedy criminals.

Meanwhile, the gang of desperate, greedy criminals had got a head start on them. Sid, Kenneth and Kenneth were sitting outside the school gates in Sid's huge, black car. Sid was keeping a beady eye out for trouble. Kenneth and Kenneth just had beady eyes.

Sid glanced up at the sky and caught sight of the red streak, then he glanced at the school gates and caught sight of Jeremy and Patsy hurrying towards the main buildings.

His brain put two and two together, made three, and added one.

"They know what's going to happen," he hissed quietly (which was probably the right thing to do this time, since our heroes might possibly have overheard him). "They must be working for the cops, or MI7, or something else disgustingly well-behaved."

The red streak was getting brighter now, and larger every second. Jeremy and Patsy could hear a high-pitched whine, getting steadily louder.

"What do we do about them, boss?" said First-Kenneth.

"Bet he says to get 'em," whispered Second-Kenneth.

"Do, gentlemen? We GET THEM!" shouted Sid. He slammed his foot down on the accelerator, and the car's wheels squealed as they spun into action. The car leaped forwards, heading straight for Jeremy and Patsy.

"Told yer," said Second-Kenneth with a

grin, clapping his hands in glee.

The car bounded past the gates at top speed. Its engine roared.

"That satellite sounds ever so near," said Jeremy, looking the other way.

Patsy spun on her heels. The car was almost upon them! No place to run! She leapt sideways, knocking Jeremy off his feet. The car screeched past, tyres missing them by millimetres. Sid hissed with anger.

"Are we going back to get them again?" said Second-Kenneth.

"No, pea-head, we're going to get to that satellite before they do!" spat Sid. The car shot on towards the school buildings.

All that blocked their way was Sharkface.

The red streak had become a flaming column of smoke. It whistled as it plummeted through the air, closer, closer.

"Of all the rotten luck," said Jeremy, dusting grass off his trousers. "A gang of desperate, greedy criminals."

Suddenly, the satellite came screaming out of the clouds, and whalloped smack through the roof of the school with a sound which can't really be put into a word but which was more or less *WHHHhhhAAAAaaammmmM*!! An explosion of dust, debris and sections of roof puffed out into the sky.

"Quick!" yelled Jeremy, standing at a slight angle, trying to look heroic. "Those villains mustn't get to it first."

Patsy's hands were pressed to the side of her head. Luckily, what she said next turned out to be completely untrue, so there's no need to worry: "I bet it's gone through about three floors. I bet there are loads of injuries and blood all over the place."

Sharkface stood in the way of Sid's car, hands on hips, sneer on face. He wasn't being brave, just plain stupid. Sid put his foot down. Sharkface tried to jump, too late. Next thing he knew, he was clinging to the car's bonnet, one hand on each headlight. The car smashed through the doors of the main building, scattering teachers and splinters of wood.

"*Aaaarrrggghhhh*!" screamed Sharkface.

The sound of the car was deafening in the corridor. Its wheels spun, and it lurched forwards, then turned a sharp left and bump-bump-bumped up the stairs.

"It's up here, and I want it!" said Sid.

"*Aaaarrrggghhhh*!" screamed Sharkface.

Jeremy flapped his arms to clear the smoke in the corridor. Patsy picked up a chunk of door, ready for a fight.

"There's no need for that," said Jeremy. "All we need is a brilliant idea to get us up a couple of floors before their car can smash its way there."

"Such as...?" said Patsy.

Kids were rapidly collecting in the corridor, their jaws hanging lower than a snake's kneecaps.

"The Chemistry lab!" said Jeremy.

"But we're both terrible at Chemistry," said Patsy. "Everything we touch explodes."

"Exactly!" Jeremy dragged a desk out of the lab, into the corridor, and put another on top of it. Then he collected a large beaker and an armful of dangerous-looking substances. "Get in between the desks," he said. He mixed all the chemicals in the beaker, and jumped in beside Patsy.

With an almighty *WHUMPH*! the mixture ignited. It was a result which would have scored Jeremy zero in an exam, but which shot two desks, one secret agent and one secret agent's best friend, through the ceiling, through another ceiling, and landed them in the Headmaster's office.

"There you are," coughed Jeremy through a cloud of dust. "Am I a genius or what?"

The car revved up another flight of stairs. Sid spun the steering wheel, and the car ploughed through a bookcase. Mr Plantaganet had been looking forward to an afternoon reading his new textbook entitled *Crop Rotation Methods In Fourteenth Century England*. He realized that he'd probably have to miss out on that particular pleasure today, since he now found himself jumping out of a hole in the wall and into the school swimming-pool.

First-Kenneth pointed a stubby finger at the kid clutching on to the bonnet of the car. "Hey, his head looks like a shark."

The car took the corner off a classroom, and a shower of plaster and falling bricks jerked it to a halt. Sharkface flew off the bonnet, out through an open window and joined Mr Plantaganet for a swim.

Sid, Kenneth and Kenneth climbed out of the vehicle.

"Spread out, boys," said Sid, coughing as the dust settled. "It's around here somewhere."

And so it was. Nearby, in the Headmaster's office, Jeremy and Patsy realized where they were, and prepared their apologies. Then they saw a large, scorched, cylindrical object, steaming gently and sitting in the spot usually occupied by the Headmaster.

"I hope that's not him," said Jeremy.

It wasn't. The Headmaster was underneath the large, scorched, cylindrical object, pinned to the floor. Origami animals were scattered all over the place. Luckily for the rest of the school, the Headmaster's stomach had broken the satellite's fall. He groaned painfully.

Jeremy and Patsy peeped over the edge of his desk and waved tiny little waves at him. They had sheepish smiles on their faces.

"Hi, Sir," said Patsy. "Give us a minute, and we'll have this out of your way."

The Headmaster's face went the red it usually reserved for major breaches of school discipline, or parents' evenings. "Kfluff mnnemm flumm ploo!" he spluttered.

"He's gone barmy," said Patsy, fearfully. "Look, he's frothing at the mouth."

"No, I think he's just swallowed half a dozen origami animals," said Jeremy.

"Or perhaps," said a sinister voice behind

them, "he's realized that the game is up."

Jeremy and Patsy spun around. Of all the things that could have happened at that point, the best would have been for Jeremy, having secretly picked up a handful of plaster dust, to fling it at the villains. They would have coughed and rubbed their eyes, allowing Jeremy and Patsy time to escape with the satellite, identify the villains to MI7, and get them picked up by the police.

Unfortunately, all Jeremy could fling was a giraffe made out of a page from an exercise book. It bounced off Second-Kenneth's nose.

"Oh, rabbits," said Patsy. "I suppose that means we're going to be captured and locked up in a dark, stinking basement in the middle of nowhere."

Chapter 3

In which our heroes are locked up in a dark, stinking basement in the middle of nowhere

....

"You just had to say it, didn't you?" grumbled Jeremy. Patsy poked her tongue out at him.

The basement was even damper and mustier than it had been on page 20, and Sid, Kenneth and Kenneth being there only made things worse. Grey-green mould grew in hideous lumps across one wall. The smell of week-old cabbage hung in the air. A bottle of Super-Strong-Ultra-Germkill Detergent would have taken one look at the grime on the floor tiles and had a screaming fit. The only light came from a tiny, smeary window, way up high above them. Jeremy and Patsy were sitting (carefully) on an upturned crate. Their left legs were chained to one of the many pipes which snaked around the walls.

Jeremy wriggled, a sour expression on his face. "I'm getting my best trousers all grubby now. And we've missed lunch."

Patsy was about to say, "Stop thinking of your stomach for once and start thinking up brilliant ideas for getting us out of this dangerous and terrifying situation!" but was interrupted by the sound of the news on the portable telly Kenneth and Kenneth were watching in the far corner. They weren't really interested in the news, they were waiting for the cartoons to come on.

"—which fell to Earth earlier today, landed safely on the stomach of Grotside School's headmaster," said the tinny voice from the telly. "The disturbance at the school was witnessed by teacher, Brian Plantaganet."

"Brian," sniggered Patsy quietly.

Mr Plantaganet appeared on the screen, dabbing his face with a towel. "There were dozens of them," he said, trembling. "They drove through school in eight bulldozers! I blocked their way as best I could, but after a long fight I was hurled through the roof. Savages, that's what they were! Maniacs!"

The newsreader came back on screen. "By the time the police arrived in a fleet of blue vans, the criminals and the satellite were long gone—"

Sid stabbed the "off" button. For a moment, the only sound was the dripping of a particularly nasty and germ-filled goo from the high ceiling. Then came the slow *K-clack K-clack* of Sid's boots as he walked over to his prisoners. Behind him, Kenneth and Kenneth quietly found a spare tape and set the video for the cartoons.

Jeremy, being a highly trained secret agent, faced Sid with a bold and steadfast expression on his face, his back straight, his mouth set in a slight sneer. Patsy, however, not being a secret agent, let her bottom lip wobble uncontrollably.

K-clack K-clack K-clack

Sid had been on the phone for the past hour. He'd worked his way through the

Baddies (International) section of Yellow Pages, and had found the phone number of the most unpleasant and disreputable computer thief in the world. The thief had been on the loo when Sid phoned, but his mum had got him to call back, and they'd settled on a price for the satellite. After he'd put the phone down, Sid had consulted his SCUM handbook, which had informed him that he should now approach his prisoners slowly, wearing noisy footwear, and say:

"Allow me to introduce myself. I am Sid Lime." The low, sinister sound of his voice bounced off the walls, found it had picked up something nasty from them, and died away.

"Good afternoon," said Jeremy politely. "I am Jeremy Brown of the Secret Service, and this is my sidekick, Patsy." Patsy kicked his side. "Sorry, this is my Executive Assistant, Patsy."

Sid gave a high-pitched cackle, as recommended in the SCUM handbook. "Secret

Service? Hah! Do they seriously believe that mere kiddies are going to stop me? I've just been on the phone to the most unpleasant and disreputable computer thief in the world, and very soon I and my colleagues here are going to be so rich they'll have to invent a new word for greedy." He gave an even higher-pitched cackle.

"They'll certainly have to invent a new word for ugly," said Jeremy.

Kenneth and Kenneth giggled, then realized he was talking about them too, and kept quiet. Sid leaned close to Jeremy, his yellowy teeth showing through a broad grin. Jeremy could smell cheese and onion crisps this time.

"My colleagues and I are now off to the rendez-vous point. By the time anyone finds you – *if* anyone finds you, that is – we'll be thousands of miles away. Come, gentlemen, we have an appointment in three hours' time. Fetch the satellite and meet me by what's left of the car."

He ushered them out, pausing only to give Jeremy and Patsy a cheery wave. If his cackle had been any higher, it would have missed his face completely. The door slammed and locked behind him with a heavy *claaanng*.

Then there was only the dripping of ooze from the ceiling.

"Oh dear," said Jeremy quietly.

Patsy kicked her leg about, making the chain rattle wildly. "Jeremy, old pal, now would be a good time to tell me that you've got a special chain-cutting type device hidden in your shoe, or a laser gun in a biro or something."

Jeremy raised an eyebrow. "Let's not be silly, Patsy."

"Can't you get MI7 on your radio?"

"We're in a basement, remember?" said Jeremy with a sigh. "That window way up there is at ground level. The signal won't reach them."

Patsy rattled her chain again, angrily. Rattling it made her feel better, so she rattled it some more. Meanwhile, Jeremy paced up and down as far as his own chain would allow. Wrapping a hankie around his hand to avoid contamination, he tapped gently at the pipework to which the other ends of their chains were attached.

"I wonder what's in these pipes?" he said, almost to himself. "If it's gas, or oil, we'll be in real trouble. Again. But if it's water..."

Patsy's freckled nose wrinkled excitedly. She could smell an escape plan taking shape, and escape plans usually meant a certain amount of noise, violence and damage to property. "What do you want me to break, J.B.?" she said, pulling up her socks and wiping her nose.

"These pipes," said Jeremy. "We'll both get dreadfully wet, of course, but that's unavoidable. *If* the pipes carry water."

Patsy's leg swung back, ready to give the pipe an almighty whack. "And if it's oil?"

"We'll come to a sticky end."

"And if it's gas?"

"We'll get blown to bits."

Patsy stuck out her bottom lip and nodded thoughtfully. "Right, better give it a really good boot, then."

She kicked the pipe. It wobbled and clanked against the wall. Another kick. It bent with a screech of metal. Another. The bend became a dent. Another. The dent became a buckle. Another. The pipe cracked and snapped in two. The chains spun free.

Jeremy and Patsy's relief that it was water which shot out was rather dampened by the fact that the water was absolutely freezing. It gushed and rushed across the basement floor, soaking everything. As it hit them, they let out howls that would have got a werewolf through to the national finals of the All England Howling Championships.

"Ha–haaaa! Who's for a swim?" yelled Patsy, a broad grin across her face. Jeremy's teeth were chattering too much for him to answer.

* * *

It took quite a while for the whole basement to fill with water, so we'll skip to the bit where Jeremy and Patsy were floating level with the window. The broken pipe was way below them, gushing silently now in the murky depths of the room.

Patsy swam over to the window with a powerful front crawl. She grabbed the frame with both hands.

"You'll have to give it a good pull, I expect," spluttered Jeremy, trying hard to keep afloat. Underwater, his arms and legs were doing a rapid doggy-paddle. "Judging from the terrible pong in this room, it hasn't been opened for years."

Patsy summoned up all her strength, then sent out for a double side order of extra, just to make sure. The water rose higher, splashing the grime-streaked pane of glass. She breathed deeply, and gripped tighter. She pulled.

Nothing.

She pushed.

Nothing.

"It won't budge!" she shrieked.

The water continued rising. There was just enough room between it and the ceiling for their heads and shoulders now.

"Try again!" called Jeremy. "The window frame's bound to be rotten through."

She gripped hard and pulled, and pushed, her face stretched tight with effort. Nothing.

"Nothing!" she yelped.

Patsy looked at Jeremy, and Jeremy looked at the window. So much for his escape plan.

"Hang on a mo," he said suddenly. He tried to doggy-paddle over to the window, but the strength of the water currents pulled him back into the centre of the room. He tried to shout to Patsy, but kept bobbing under the surface. All he could do was make a turning motion with his hands.

"Huh?" said Patsy, frowning. She was having trouble keeping afloat herself. The water was fast approaching the ceiling, and the muck on the ceiling was making the water wish it had never left the pipe in the first place.

Then Patsy realized what Jeremy meant. She felt along the window frame, found a tiny little catch, and flipped it open.

Water gushed out into the open air, and the two of them gushed along with it.

They were in a scruffy, weed-covered and now soaking wet courtyard. They staggered to their feet, coughing and trying to ignore the horrible smells that were clinging to their clothes. Patsy gave a thumbs-up sign. "That was fun!" she said breathlessly.

Jeremy tried to smooth his hair back into place, and actually did quite a good job of it. "I really am quite frighteningly clever," he said. "Did I ever tell you about the time I escaped from a pit of poisonous snakes using only a rubber band, a silk handkerchief and a positive attitude?"

"Yes," said Patsy. "Call MI7, quick. The satellite could be anywhere by now."

Jeremy pulled out the hidden aerial of his communicator. "Ooo, ow!" He shook both thumbs a couple of times. "No good, it's completely waterlogged. We're on our own."

Patsy shook herself like a dog. "Oh, rabbits. There must be some way of knowing where they've gone. The ratty little one said they had a meeting in three hours. He also said they'd be thousands of miles away soon."

They stood and thought carefully for a moment.

Chapter 4

In which our heroes have worked out that the answer is the airport

....

"Your attention, please." A crisp, female voice echoed around the polished halls and corridors of Terminal One. "This is an important announcement. Will all passengers tronpolling on the glumpy plinky plonky, make sure that flumpy dinky doo, bim bom pilly clump. Thank you." The airport announcer had no idea why they made her say such things. It's a well-known fact that airport announcements sound like gobbledegook. Less well known is the fact that they *are*.

Jeremy and Patsy had put on dark glasses in an effort to look more official and dangerous. Their clothes were crumpled and damp, so the effort was completely wasted, but they reckoned they looked pretty cool in shades, so they kept them on.

"We must try to blend in and be as inconspicuous as possible," whispered Jeremy. He straightened his tie, which was now all twisted and curly, and they looked around at the shifting crowds of passengers and the blinking display screens.

"I can't see the blinking display screens 'cos of these blinking glasses," mumbled Patsy.

"Whassall this then?" said a low voice beside Jeremy's right ear. Jeremy almost jumped out of his skin, but didn't, thanks to his knowledge of the MI7 leaflet, "How Not To Jump Out Of Your Skin". They turned, to find a dozen security guards looming over them, with their long truncheons and short tempers at the ready.

"You are herewith looking of a highly suspicious and non-passenger-style nature," said another guard.

"My name is Jeremy Brown," said Jeremy correctly, "and this is my – Operations

Director, Patsy Spudd. Glad to see you chaps are on the ball. Now, if you'll run along, we're on official business of a highly sensitive and non-airport-style nature."

The guard with the narrowest eyes and the widest nose leaned closer. He sniffed Jeremy, and his eyes suddenly widened in disgust. "If you're on official business, sonny Jim, then I'm the Queen of Sheba."

"We'd love to stay and chat, Your Majesty, really we would," said Jeremy, "but we've got important work to do, catching a gang of international computer thieves."

Unfortunately, if there was one thing the security guards wouldn't stand for, it was someone else doing the chasing of villains in their airport. All together, they snatched pairs of handcuffs from their belts and flipped them open. "You're coming with us!" they all bellowed.

Fortunately, if there was one thing that Jeremy Brown was famed for at MI7, it was having amazing pieces of good luck at moments like this. The amazing piece of good luck he had at this particular moment involved a large crowd of Japanese tourists sweeping past, allowing him and Patsy to conceal themselves among the luggage and souvenir hats. By the time the guards had stopped answering questions about where to find the check-in desks and the toilets, Jeremy and Patsy had long gone.

They sneaked away from the crowd just in time to avoid being put on a non-stop overnight flight to Okinawa. (Patsy had made several friends, and swapped addresses and photos with a Mr and Mrs Kawamishi from Tokyo.) They headed off towards the departure lounge.

"Keep a look-out for a large rucksack," said Jeremy, "or something else large and travel-related that they might have stashed the satellite in. Even that lot aren't so stupid as to carry millions of pounds worth of stolen high technology on open view through a public place."

First-Kenneth was dragging millions of pounds worth of stolen high technology across the floor towards the check-in desks. He was struggling because it weighed almost three tonnes, and because heat-scarred bits of its outer casing kept getting caught on the carpet. Second-Kenneth was too busy hitching up his trousers to help. It was Second-Kenneth's belt that his brother was using as a rope with which to drag the satellite.

Sid had gone to the third phone booth from the left, next to the queue for Flight DH103 to Spain, as he had been instructed. He had dialled the number he'd been told to memorize, and had now been informed by the most unpleasant and disreputable computer thief in the world's mum exactly where the plane would be waiting for them.

He returned to Kenneth and Kenneth.

"Gentlemen," he said quietly, his eyes darting in all directions to make sure nobody was sneaking up on them.

"Can you see all right with your eyes like that, boss?" said Second-Kenneth.

"Shut up. Everything is arranged. We now go to the departure lounge and wait for a contact to contact us. We will board the private jet of the most unpleasant and disreputable computer thief in the world, we will be given a quite disgustingly large sum of money, and then his mum says it's OK to get a lift to Brazil. Oh, and we're to make sure he's wearing his woolly jumper. He got wet today, apparently, and he might have caught a chill."

They arrived at the departure lounge in the space of one short sentence. The satellite bumped along behind First-Kenneth, leaving a trail of little bits of metal behind it. Second-Kenneth scampered off to the shops to get some comics and dolly mixture for the journey, and Sid found somewhere to sit away from the law-abiding folk.

Jeremy and Patsy, crawling along on their

hands and knees to keep out of sight of the gang, were soon positioned underneath Sid's chair. The alert reader will have already worked out how our heroes had tracked the gang down. Any readers who are not alert have jolly well missed out now.

"Lucky you told them this gizmo was a shaving kit," dribbled Second-Kenneth through a mouthful of liquorice (the shop had sold out of dolly mixtures), "or we might not have got it through customs."

"If we bring their buyer to justice," whispered Jeremy, "we could deal a deadly blow to world computer crime."

"Or at least give it a good poke in the eye," whispered Patsy.

"I'd be famous!" whispered Jeremy.

"No, I'd be famous. You're a secret agent."

"Oh yeh."

They didn't have long to wait. A figure wearing a long, dark raincoat, black gloves and a wide-brimmed hat to keep his face in shadow, walked briskly past. He looked every inch the despicable low-life, and Sid was dead jealous.

"This way," said the figure, a hankie held to his mouth to disguise his voice. Jeremy only caught a brief glimpse of him, but noticed that there was definitely something shark-shaped about his head.

Sid jumped up. From their hiding place, Jeremy and Patsy saw a sudden confusion of three pairs of feet.

"Come along, gentlemen. Careful with the merchandise. Oh, for heaven's sake leave the sweeties, you can get some more later."

The feet hurried away, followed by the heavy dragging sound of the satellite.

"Red alert, Patsy!"

They scrambled out and followed, hurrying from doorway to waste bin, waste bin to behind-the-corner, behind-the-corner to behind-somebody's newspaper. The gang were led out of the terminal building, and on to the vast, open stretch of concrete which led, in turn, to the airport's runways.

From around the corner of the terminal building came an unmarked aeroplane, its jet engines shrieking, ready for take-off. It was much smaller than those used to take tourists on holiday. Jeremy, concealed by a security patrol car, estimated it would seat about two dozen people.

"So with Fatty and Fatty II: The Sequel, it'll be quite a squash," yelled Patsy above the din.

The plane taxied slowly in a wide circle. The howling of the engines rose and fell as it manoeuvred. The mysterious figure stepped forward, holding his hat on to his head, and beckoned to the gang. A door in the side of the plane swung open, and a short stepladder dropped out. It was soon fixed, and the villains boarded the plane. At least, two of them boarded the plane, the other two sort of squeezed in painfully, grunting and wriggling.

"Now! We can't let them get away!" yelled Jeremy.

The door began to close, and the plane began to glide towards the runway. Patsy broke cover and dashed towards it. Jeremy broke cover and decided that running after the thing was just too much effort.

A security guard approached the patrol car they'd been hiding behind, and hopped into the driver's seat. Jeremy hopped in beside him.

"Follow that plane!" he ordered.

"I can't do that," said the guard, "I'll be in trouble."

The plane was getting further away. Patsy's trainers pounded the tarmac. Her face was redder than her hair, and her arms shifted faster than a fresh batch of hot cakes.

"Quick!" said Jeremy. "Follow that plane!"

"Ooo, are you a secret agent or something?" said the guard excitedly.

"I can't tell you that, it's a secret!"

"Oh, go on, don't be rotten."

The plane's engines were picking up speed.

"Just drive!" yelled Jeremy.

The guard drove.

"You're not like the other guards, are you?"

said Jeremy.

"No," said the guard sadly, "we don't get on very well."

The patrol car drew level with Patsy. If she'd been able to spare the time and energy to make a rude sign at Jeremy, she would have.

Faces appeared at the plane's windows. Sid looked horrified and shouted something to the pilot. The two Kenneths squashed their noses against the glass and puffed out their cheeks.

Patsy leaped forward, flinging herself on to the plane's wing. Her legs flapped madly as she fought to keep a grip on the smooth surface.

Jeremy wound down the window and clambered out on to the roof of the patrol car. The wind blew his hair into a frizzy mass, but there was no time to worry about that now. The guard swerved the patrol car nervously as Jeremy, flat on his stomach, crossed the roof. He pulled up his knees, steadied himself, and jumped.

He skidded across the wing. The plane was veering left and right in an effort to shake them off. Patsy caught his collar as he began to slip backwards. "Didn't I say I always have to save you?" she grumbled.

The door in the side of the plane *kss-chunged* as it unlocked and swung open. Kenneth (they couldn't tell which one) stuck his head out. "Hallo," he said with a little wave, "nice to see you again."

Sid kicked him from behind. "No it isn't!" he hissed. "Tell them to buzz off!"

"Buzz off," said Kenneth.

"No!" said Jeremy defiantly.

Sid's cackle was almost as loud as the engines. The door shut and bolted. The plane picked up speed, moving out on to the runway. It accelerated, faster and faster. Jeremy and Patsy gripped the wing with all their strength. Their eyes were tightly shut against the wind. The runway shot past under their feet. The whine of the engines rose higher and higher. The plane's nose rocked slightly. The runway seemed to drop away beneath them. The plane banked steeply upwards. Their stomachs suddenly rolled over and did a couple of double somersaults that any Olympic gymnast would have been proud of.

Kenneth and Kenneth watched calmly from inside. Second-Kenneth munched on a packet of wine gums. One day he'd learn to take the wine gums out first.

The plane gained altitude. Patsy's hands were frozen with cold and her face ached from being screwed up so hard.

"I— think—," she screamed at Jeremy, "when— they— said— buzz— off— you— should— have— said— YYEEEEESSSS!!"

Chapter 5

In which everybody gets duffed up and our heroes face certain death

....

Inside the plane, Sid dodged this way and that to see around the Kenneths. "What are they doing?" he said. "Why aren't they falling off?"

"That ginger lass is a strong 'un," murmured First-Kenneth to his brother. "I'd like her to be my girlfriend."

"Well get out there and tell her, then!" spat Sid through gritted teeth.

"Huh?" said the Kenneths. Their jaws dangled.

"Get out on the wing and throw them off!" said Sid. "We've come too far to let a couple of do-gooders spoil things!" He turned, grinning weakly and bowing to the most unpleasant and disreputable computer thief in the world, who was sitting at the far end of the cabin. "Don't you agree, Your Most Wonderful Nastiness, Sir?" he squirmed.

The computer thief smiled a dreary smile.

Sid unlocked the door and flung it open. Howling blasts of air suddenly filled the cabin.

The first Jeremy and Patsy knew about Sid's plan was when two huge, heavy shapes thumped on to the wing in front of them. The plane spun to one side, the weight of all four of them pulling it over.

The Kenneths screamed for their mum. The ground, far below them, appeared to flip up and round and over their heads, and up and round and over as the plane rolled.

Jeremy and Patsy screamed for their mums too.

The Kenneths, holding on tightly, struck out. A fat palm smacked against Jeremy's shoulder and he let go with one hand. He fluttered like a shirt on a washing line. Patsy ducked to avoid a flying fist. She was sure she could hear someone shouting about going out for a pizza sometime, but decided she must be going barmy.

The plane stabilized, but on its side. The weight of the Kenneths kept the wing they were on pointing downwards, with the other wing sticking up vertically. Patsy glanced down for a second, then wished she hadn't. They were about 10,000 feet off the ground.

A fat fist smacked against Jeremy's fingers. Luckily, the fingers were so cold by now that the blow wasn't too painful, and he managed to hang on. Then a boot squashed into his face. His fingers were at full stretch. His mouth twisted sideways as the boot pushed harder.

Patsy's grip was being reduced a bit at a time. First-Kenneth grabbed each of her fingers in turn and pulled them off the surface of the wing. "One little piggie went to Margate..." called First-Kenneth. "One little piggie sat in foam..."

Jeremy yelled as loud as the boot would

allow: "Hey, boys! Who wants an ice-cream?!"

The Kenneths both jumped up and down in excitement, then realized they were jumping up and down in mid-air. They found themselves watching the ground getting closer and closer.

With their weight gone, the plane flipped through one hundred and eighty degrees. Jeremy and Patsy's grip on the wing finally gave out and they, too, fell. But with the plane now the other way up, they fell straight in through the door. The plane twisted again and flew level.

Wind whipped around the cabin. Jeremy and Patsy painfully untangled themselves from the Eazee-Rest reclining seats, and stared up into Sid's weaselly face.

"Oh, I'm really, really unhappy now," said Sid quietly.

Jeremy clambered to his feet and tried to look dignified. "I order you to turn this plane around and return to the airport!"

"Shan't!" said Sid.

"Since they refuse to let us dispose of them," said a weary voice from the other end of the cabin, "they will have to come with us. We have many friends where we're going. They won't escape all of them."

Both Jeremy and Patsy knew that voice instantly.

There were lots of reasons why Jeremy liked being a secret agent. There was the thrill of bringing dangerous villains to justice, there was the joy of not being at school. There was also, now and again, the chance to be totally and completely gobsmacked by something. As the owner of the voice stood up and stepped forward, Jeremy could honestly say that his gob had never been more smacked. The mysterious figure at the airport had been Sharkface – definitely. However, the most unpleasant and dis-reputable computer thief in the world now turned out to be...

"Mr Plantaganet!" said Jeremy.

"Crumbs," said Patsy, peeking over the back of a seat.

"You're not the only one with a secret identity," said Mr Plantaganet dolefully. "I did a college course in computer piracy long ago, and with this," he pointed to the satellite, strapped firmly into a seat, "I can hack into any system anywhere in the world. Nothing will be safe. Not banks, not building society current accounts. I'll have access to money, anybody's and everybody's, whenever I want it."

Sid had read about this in the SCUM handbook – the big villain's revealing speech to the good guys, just before the end. He was filled with admiration. Then he frowned. Just before the end?

"Wait a minute!" he cried. "You're not getting *my* money!" The suitcase crammed with cash that Mr Plantaganet had given him in exchange for the satellite was wedged into the luggage rack overhead. Over Jeremy's head, fortunately. Jeremy yanked it free, intending to hold it up above him heroically, but it weighed a tonne. It thudded to the floor instead.

"Leave that alone, Brown!" cried Mr Plantaganet, with a weary sweep of his hand. "I've got to double-cross this little creep yet and steal it back!"

"*What*??!" yelled Sid.

"You pushed me into a swimming-pool, you oaf!"

"Aha! You're not wearing your woolly jumper! I'm telling your mum!"

Jeremy kicked the case over and gave it a shove. It slid to the very edge of the open doorway. Sid and Mr Plantaganet both dived for it at the same time. Patsy pulled off a shoe and flung it hard. It hit the case, which toppled out into space, and the villains toppled out with it.

They fell trying to thump each other. The suitcase was snatched from one to the other and back again, as they shrank to tiny dots in the distance.

"I'm puzzled," said Jeremy. "That was Sharkface at the airport. Where did he go, then?"

"Look out!" yelled Patsy.

Sharkface sprang from the cockpit. He ripped a seat off its metal runners, and hurled it. They dropped to the floor and it crashed into the wall behind them.

"I suppose you've been the one piloting this thing," said Jeremy. Sharkface ripped up another seat.

"You're that snotty little Brown nobody from school," he grunted.

"I am Jeremy Brown of the Secret Service, and you're under arrest!"

Another seat smashed against the wall. Sharkface leapt at Jeremy. All Jeremy could think of was what had happened that morning on the way to school. He wasn't going to let it happen again. As Sharkface lunged for his throat, he ducked and rolled on to his back. Sharkface was going too fast to stop. He flew over Jeremy's head, and out through the door.

"That's that, then," said Jeremy.

Wrong.

The plane suddenly dipped sharply and went into a dive. The ground appeared through the front window, and the screaming of the engines rose to a deafening screech. Jeremy and Patsy tumbled forwards into the cockpit.

"Quick!" shouted Patsy. "Pull it up straight!"

Jeremy jumped into the pilot's seat and strapped himself in. His fingers fluttered over the dozens of switches and levers and displays in front of him. "Er..."

"You can fly a plane, can't you?" said Patsy. "I mean, Sharkface can fly a plane – *could* fly a plane. You must have done 'How To Fly A Plane' at MI7, surely?"

"That's next week," muttered Jeremy with a trembling voice.

"So this is it, then! After all that, we're still facing certain death!"

This time, one of Patsy's doom-laden remarks looked like being completely correct.

Jeremy grabbed the joystick in front of him and pulled hard. No response. He searched the displays for useful information. The ground was getting closer every second. A red light above a row of other red lights blinked: AUTOPILOT LOCKED. SECURITY CODE REQUIRED FOR RELEASE.

"Our history teacher taught Sharkface a trick or two, anyway," said Jeremy. "They've made sure that if they didn't make it, neither would we!"

"Would breaking anything help?" asked Patsy hopefully.

"No, no, no! Get the satellite!" said Jeremy. "We've been chasing it around all day, the least it can do for us is a few sums!"

Patsy struggled back up the cabin, which was now almost vertical. The engines howled, and the rushing air made the remaining seats shake violently. She unstrapped the satellite. The second the buckle was unfastened, the weight of the thing sent her (and it) crashing back into the cockpit.

"Don't damage it!" yelled Jeremy.

Patsy would have given him a poke in the eye if she hadn't been pinned flat against the control panel. Jeremy opened several hatches in the side of the satellite, unwound the electric leads that fell out, and searched for a suitable socket among the plane's controls, in front of him.

"The good thing about this technology stuff," he mumbled, "is that these days you can... Ahah!"

He plugged in. Patsy looked out of the window, then wished she hadn't. They couldn't have been more than five thousand feet off the ground now.

A screen came to life on the side of the satellite. As words appeared on it, a high, calm voice echoed them from a tiny speaker on the plane's control panel. "Initializing... Initializing..."

"Come on," mumbled Jeremy.

"Initialization stage complete," said the satellite gently. "Status now being checked."

"We're going to crash!! That's our bloomin' status!!" bellowed Patsy.

"Patsy, be cool," said Jeremy, very, very worried indeed.

"Status check complete," said the satellite calmly. "Altitude now 4,976 feet and falling... 4,532 feet and falling... 3,991 feet and falling... Speed beyond tolerance levels. Evasive action recommended."

"Well do it, then!" shouted Patsy.

"You can't just tell it, Patsy, you have to program it."

"3,433 feet."

Clouds flashed past the windows. Patsy could make out buildings down below. Her stomach said a quick toodle-oo and tried to find the nearest exit. Jeremy tapped uselessly at the keyboard set into the side of the satellite. It was at this point that he wished he'd payed more attention during Computer Science.

"2,877 feet," said the satellite. "Evasive action required. Impact in seventeen seconds... sixteen... fifteen..."

"Shut up!!" screamed Patsy.

Jeremy clapped his hands to his head. He had to think. They both had to think. Thinking was the only way out.

"twelve... eleven... ten seconds..."

"The satellite's monitoring the plane's controls now," murmured Jeremy quickly. "The controls are locked. If the satellite realizes they're locked, it'll take them over."

"nine... eight... seven..."

Startled birds clung to the plane's nose, squawking. Patsy could see trees, fields, cars on the roads.

"six... five..."

Jeremy pulled hard on the joystick. The satellite bleeped.

"Controls disabled," it said soothingly. "Autopilot overridden. Safety program running."

Suddenly, the plane's nose lurched

upwards. Gravitational forces pulled Jeremy and Patsy tight into their seats. The plane swooped in a sharp U-shape. The tip of the left wing clipped a spray of leaves from a tree. The sudden falling of a whopping great aircraft, and its lightning manoeuvres back up into the sky, made a nearby flock of sheep jump out of their fleeces. Most of them would be taking pills for their nerves for the rest of their lives, but at least justice had been done, and a disaster averted.

As the plane automatically banked and headed back to the airport, Jeremy took out a hankie, mopped his brow, and had clearly forgotten all about the "How To Stop Shaking Like A Leaf" lesson MI7 had given him.

"Looks like I've saved the day again," he said cheerily.

Patsy socked him across the jaw, but he took no notice.

"Did I ever tell you about the time I fooled a Russian assassin into thinking he was a small dog called Arnold?"

"Yes," said Patsy crossly.

The concerned and sensitive reader will be pleased to hear that none of those ejected at 10,000 feet ended up as a blob of strawberry jam on someone's front doorstep. As the plane came safely in to land, Sid, the Kenneths, Mr Plantaganet and Sharkface were crawling safely out of the sludge tanks at the sewage works and into the welcoming arms of the airport security guards.

Jeremy and Patsy returned home. They trudged up the street towards their respective houses.

"I'm going to have a bath," said Jeremy. "I'm going to put these vilely stained clothes in the wash, and I'm going to prepare a new chapter for my memoirs, entitled 'I Foiled Crime At 10,000 Feet'."

Patsy said something very rude indeed, but Jeremy wasn't listening because there was a buzzing sensation in his left thumb...